Everyone...

Christopher Silas Neal

CANDLEWICK PRESS

Sometimes . . .

the day never seems to end.

You might be happy

one moment

and sad the next.

Or frustrated,

frazzled,

fed up,

bonkers,

batty,

bananas . . .

Ahhhhhh!

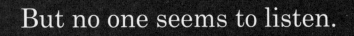

But no one seems to listen.

Sometimes, you just need to cry,
and that's OK.

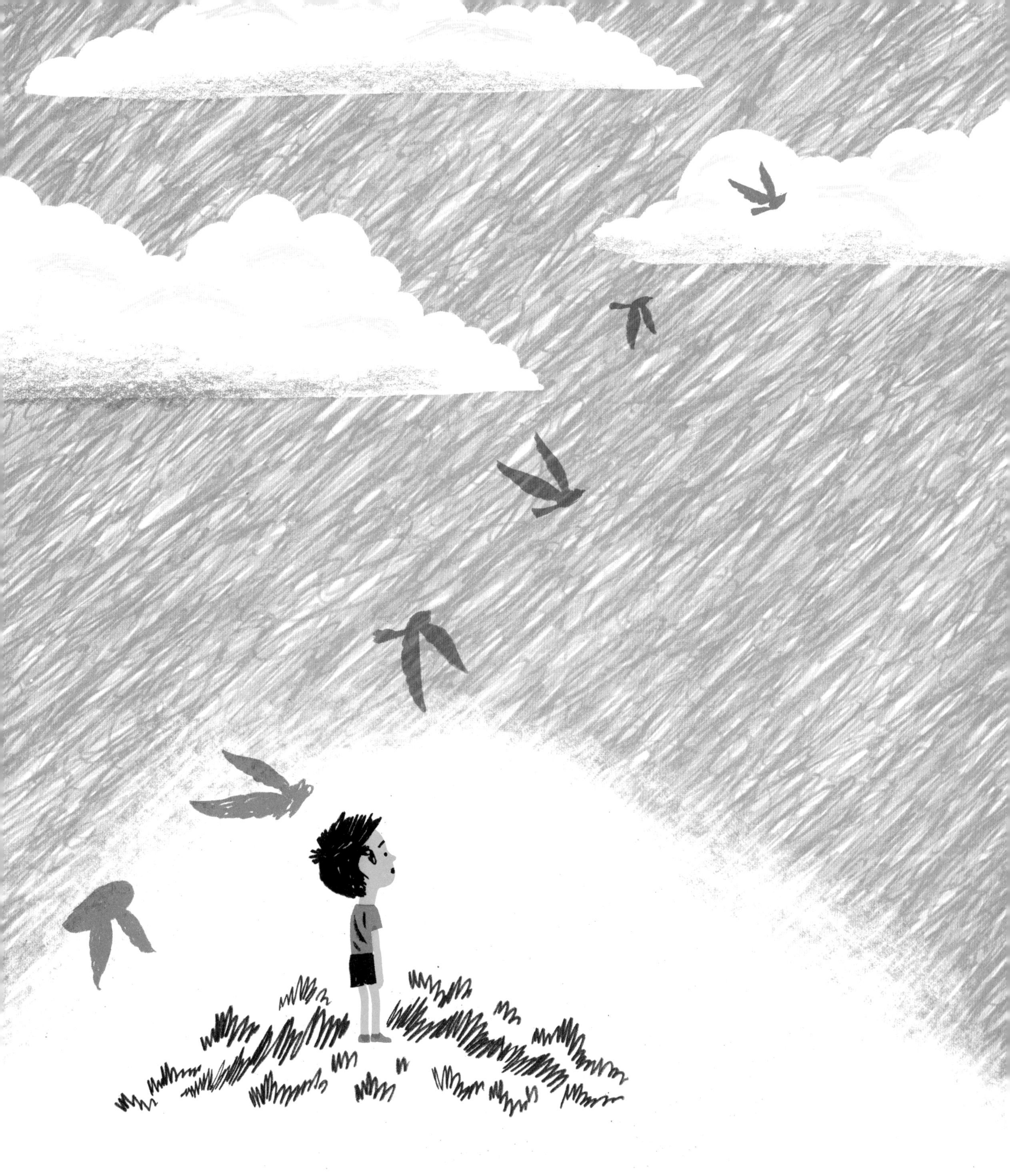

When you cry, you are not alone.

When you laugh . . .

happiness

grows.

And when you sing . . .

everyone listens.

Everyone sings,

everyone laughs,

everyone cries every now and then.

Everyone has feelings, and that's OK.

Because everyone shares them. . . .

Everyone.

For Jasper Silas Neal

First edition 2016

Library of Congress Catalog Card Number 2015934394
ISBN 978-0-7636-7683-4

16 17 18 19 20 21 CCP 10 9 8 7 6 5 4 3 2 1

Printed in Shenzhen, Guangdong, China

This book was typeset in Century Schoolbook.
The illustrations were done in mixed media.

Candlewick Press
99 Dover Street
Somerville, Massachusetts 02144

visit us at www.candlewick.com